# Hi, I'm An Insect
## Insects Among Us

By: John L. Brown
Copyright © 2021 By: John L. Brown

Hi, i'm an insect, my name is Assassin Bug, is that a weird name or what? I will tell you somethings about us. We are predatory insects that are of great benefit to gardeners. We are proficient at capturing and feeding on a wide variety of prey including other bugs, bees, flies, and caterpillars. Prey are captured with a quick stab of the assassin bug's long mouthparts. Real scary.

I'm a very ugly creature, I look like a stick or a branch of a tree. My name is Walking stick, but I go by Sticky, which sounds much better. Let me tell you something about us. We are a group of highly camouflaged insects. We escape predation by blending into plant material. As our name suggests, they look just like sticks, and may even sway back and forth to more closely resemble a twig moving in the wind.

Bat Bug's my name and don't forget it. Want to know a little more about us? We are members of the Cimicidae family of insects. We're actually relatives to another household pest — the common bed bug. Unlike the common bed bug, however, bat bugs do not prefer to feed on human blood, though they will if need be. However, as their name suggests, their first choice of food is bat blood.

They call me Cutworm, I know it's funny, but that's my name. I will tell you about us. We're a moderate-sized moth with a wingspan of about 1.5 inches in size. We have a dark brown back, with the outside third lighter. Markings on the forewing are, for the most part, indistinct. I hope you see me someday.

Booklice here, say that ten times real fast. Here's the scoop on us. We are small, pale-brown colored lice that are often found eating up old, moldy books. That's how we got our name. Although we're not considered true lice, we have the appearance, size, and shape of lice. We are common in the typical household and aren't that difficult to control.

Carpet Beetle here. I think you're going to be watching out for me in your carpet now. Here's my story. We carpet beetles damage results from larvae eating holes into natural fiber items like wool, silk, feathers, dead insects, and leather. We immature pests also have bristly hairs that can irritate skin. When we mature into adults, we feed on pollen instead of fabric items.

They call us Deer ticks, or blacklegged ticks, and we are very small, blood sucking insects. We prefer to feed on larger animals, such as deer, but we will also bite humans. We can spread the bacteria that causes Lyme disease, though we may also carry other bacteria. I like the name Ticky better, don't you? I know everyone is afraid of me because I can call Lyme disease, but I won't hurt you, I promise.

Filbert Weevil. Hi everyone. We're a species of weevil in the genus Curculio. We are considered a pest for many species of oak tree due to the damage we cause to acorns. I'm very sorry we do damage to oak trees. We don't mean to hurt oak trees but we have to eat. I do like to eat.

Flea beetles, and we're are small. We have a shiny-coat with large rear legs, which allow us to jump like fleas when threatened. There are many species of us. Some species attack a wide range of plants, while others target only certain plant families. My real name is Fleavy, cool name isn't it?

Giant water bugs are oval-shaped, with pincer-like front appendages that capture and hold prey. Our rear legs are especially flattened and have tiny hairs to help propel us through the water. Wow, even I didn't know that about us. I think I'm smart but after reading this, I need more learning. Joe the giant water bug.

The giant Weta is the world's heaviest reported insect. It can weigh up to 2.5 ounces, though many Weta don't reach quite that giant of proportions. ITS NAME MEANS "GOD OF UGLY THINGS." The name Weta comes from the Maori word Wetapunga, or "god of ugly things." The genus name, deinacrida, means "terrible grasshopper." I don't know what to say about the Giant Weta, but it's a nice big name.

I'm creepy, and my name is Head Lice, scary? We hold tightly to hair with hook-like claws at the end of each of our six legs. Head lice nits are cemented firmly to the hair shaft and can be difficult to remove even after the nymphs hatch and empty casings remain. I'm sure glad I don't have hair on my head.

The Hercules beetle, that's me, is a species of rhinoceros beetle native to the rainforests of Central America, South America, and the Lesser Antilles. It is the longest extant species of beetle in the world, and is also one of the largest flying insects in the world. I'm strong don't you think so?

The hummingbird-hawk-moth species is named for its similarity to hummingbirds, as they feed on the nectar of tube-shaped flowers using their long proboscis while hovering in the air; this resemblance is an example of convergent evolution. I would like to be call Hawk. It sounds better. I'm not a hummingbird, I don't hum.

Japanese beetles are an invasive species. Japanese beetles feed on the leaves, flowers or fruit of more than 300 species of plants. Japanese beetle grubs are pests of turfgrass. They chew grass roots, causing the turf to brown and die. I can speak English if you prefer. They call me Jasper man. I like it much better because it's shorter.

They call me Kissing Bug. We're also called cone-nosed bugs, bloodsuckers, cinches, and triatomine bugs. Like mosquitoes and ticks, we need blood to live. We usually suck it from animals, including dogs, but sometimes we bite people. We hide during the day and come out at night to eat. Everthing above really sounds bad, but I'm not really that mean. Do you think I'm that mean?

Leafhoppers get their name from their impressive jumping ability, which aids their escape when disturbed. In addition to feeding damage, some leafhoppers also transmit pathogens that cause plant disease. Several generations of these pests may occur each year. I really like my name Leaf Hooper, but for all of the above, we're sorry.

"Mite" What a name! Now there's name I can have. Mite is a term commonly used to refer to a group of insect-like organisms, some of which bite or cause irritation to humans. While some mites parasitize animals, including man, others are scavengers, some feed on plants, and many prey on insects and other arthropods. My name sounds like I'm very big, but I'm not.

I'm a Pharaoh Ant, and I'm very small, about 1/16-inch long. We are colored light yellow to red, with black markings on the abdomen. We look similar to Thief Ants, but Pharoah Ants have three segments in the antennal club. Since we are so tiny, we can travel and trail to many places. Cool little booger if I say so myself.

The scorpion fly is a strange-looking insect that is found in gardens
and hedgerows, and along woodland edges, particularly among
Stinging nettles and bramble. It has a long, beak-like projection
from its head that it uses to feed. It scavenges on dead insects and
frequently steals the contents of spiders' webs. The name may scare
you but don't worry, I'll try not to hurt you.

The American spider beetle is about 1.5 to 3.5 millimeters in length. These are the spider beetles most often confused with bed bugs because, seen from above, their body shape is similar to that of a bed bug. They are also reddish brown in color, much like adult bed bugs. At least I'm from America. I know most of you are scared of spiders, but I'm a spider beetle.

Stink bugs get their name from the unpleasant odor they produce when they are threatened. It is thought that this odor helps protect the bugs against predators. The stink bugs produce the smelly chemical in a gland on their abdomen. Some species can actually spray the chemical several inches. Please don't call me stink bug, how would you like to be called stink bug?

Termites feed on dead plants and trees. Termites get nutrients from cellulose, an organic fiber found in wood and plant matter. Subterranean termites prefer softwoods, but may invade most species of wood. Dampwood termites generally stay close to the ground, but will choose moist, decaying wood anywhere it is found. Termite makes me sound much bigger than I am.

The titan beetle is the largest known beetle in the Amazon rain forest and one of the largest insect species in the world. Adult titan beetles can grow up to 6.5 inches in length. They defend themselves against predators by using their sharp spines and strong jaws.
Wow! I'm a big bug man. I'm much bigger than most insects haha.